Word List

Here is a list of words that might make it easier
to read this book. You'll find them in boldface
the first time they appear in the story.

hover	HUH-ver
Modans	MOH-dans
telekinesis	te-li-kuh-NEE-suhs
telepathy	tuh-LE-puh-thee
newcomers	NOO-kuhm-erz
Cosmos	KOZ-mohs
crisis	KREYE-suhs
polluting	puh-LOO-ting
geologist	jee-AH-luh-jist
Rados	RAY-dohs
educational	e-juh-KAY-shuh-nuhl
rhyming	REYEM-ing
diagrams	DEYE-uh-grams
evacuate	i-VA-kyuh-wayt

BARBIE and associated trademarks are owned by and used under
license from Mattel, Inc. © 1999 Mattel, Inc. All Rights Reserved.
Published by Grolier Books, a division of Grolier Enterprises, Inc.
Story by Joanne Barkan. Photo crew: Herve Grison, Mary Hirahara, Dave Bateman,
Tim Geison, Susan Cracraft, Damon Dulas, Lisa Collins, and Judy Tsuno.
Produced by Bumpy Slide Books.
Printed in the United States of America.
ISBN: 0-7172-8890-0

GROLIER
B O O K S

Chapter One

Stacie looked up at the sun-star in the orange sky. Her stomach grumbled.

"I don't just *feel* hungry," she said to her friend Janet. "I *sound* hungry!"

"Me, too," Janet agreed. "I wish the **hover** bus would get here. As soon as we're home, I'm having a cosmic-size snack."

It was the year 2190 on the planet Moda-5. Stacie and Janet stood outside North Galaxy School with the other students. Stacie and Janet were Humans. They wore tights, astroboots, and loose-fitting, hip-length tops called tunics. The rest of the students were **Modans.** They wore long, shiny robes that covered their arms and legs. Only their heads and pink hair could be seen. The boys had purple skin, and the girls had blue-green skin. Modans didn't walk. They glided along without ever touching the ground.

"There it is!" someone shouted.

An oval-shaped school bus moved toward them. It had no wheels. Instead, it coasted along

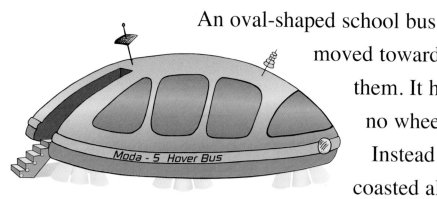

Moda - 5 Hover Bus

the road silently, six inches above the ground. It stopped in front of the students. A door opened, and a set of stairs came down. All the children leapt forward.

"Hey, quit shoving!" one Human complained.

"Ouch!" squealed a Modan.

The deep voice of the robot bus driver

scolded them. "Pupils will please practice proper manners."

Stacie, Janet, and a Modan classmate reached the bus door last. The Modan girl glided onto the bus. As Stacie stepped up, her mini-videophone slipped out of her pocket. The Modan turned and saw the phone fall. The instant she looked at it, the phone stopped in midair. Then it swooped up and hovered in front of Stacie.

Modans could move things without ever touching them. They did it by concentrating on the energy fields that surround objects. This process was called **telekinesis.**

"Too bad you Humans can't use your *minds* to catch things," the Modan girl laughed in a squeaky, babyish voice. "It's so-o-o easy."

Stacie grabbed her videophone out of the air. "Too bad you Modans all talk like babies," she shot back. "It sounds so-o-o silly."

The robot driver's voice boomed again,

3

"Pupils will please practice politeness."

Stacie sighed. "Thanks for catching my phone," she mumbled to the Modan girl.

Stacie and Janet moved to the back of the bus. They sat behind two Modan boys who were staring at each other. Now and then the boys would laugh. A small rubber ball bounced on the floor between them. But the boys' hands were nowhere in sight. The Modans were using their minds to make the ball bounce.

Stacie watched the Modan boys. "Sometimes I wish I could do that," she whispered to Janet. She pointed to the bouncing rubber ball.

"Yuck!" Janet whispered back. "Then you'd be *Modan*, not Human. You'd have that weird Modan 'accent'. And you'd talk like a big baby."

Stacie nodded in agreement.

Janet frowned and added, "And I hate it when Modans talk to each other without words. They call it **telepathy.** I call it rude. I always feel

4

like they're talking about me."

Stacie didn't say anything else. She was thinking about Modans and Humans. Modans had always lived on Moda-5. Then, a hundred  years ago, the first Humans had arrived. They had come from a far-off planet called Earth in a galaxy called the Milky Way.

The Humans had wanted to study telepathy and telekinesis. Modan children learned these difficult skills by age four. The Human visitors had never succeeded in learning the skills. But they had liked Moda-5 and settled on the planet. A hundred years later, Humans were still thought of as "**newcomers.**" And they made up a quarter

5

of the planet's population. Humans and Modans worked together. Their children went to school together. Yet the two groups lived in different neighborhoods. In general, Humans and Modans just didn't get along.

"**Cosmos** Plaza!" the robot driver called out.

Janet nudged Stacie. "Come on. It's our stop."

Cosmos Plaza was the large square in the center of town. Cactus plants decorated the square. The plaza had no trees or grass, because Moda-5 was a desert planet. The two girls hopped off the hover bus and ran past benches. They dodged robots selling snacks and sweeping the street.

The girls reached the big fountain in the center of the square. They stopped to catch their breath. They looked at the stone statues and huge empty fountain.

"I wish there was more water on this planet," Janet sighed. "I love this fountain. But it has been dry for a long time."

"It's been a year since the water **crisis** really hit," Stacie pointed out. "Everyone had been wasting water and **polluting** it for too long. Now there's hardly any left."

The friends walked the rest of the way across Cosmos Plaza.

"Do you think anyone will ever discover a new source of water for Moda-5?" Janet asked.

Stacie looked worried. "Barbie says the scientists haven't found anything yet," she answered. Barbie was Stacie's older sister. She worked as a **geologist.** That meant she studied rocks.

"Barbie says we have enough water for one more year. But we will have to find more somewhere else in the galaxy," Stacie explained.

"What if we don't?" asked Janet.

"If not, everyone will have to leave Moda-5. We'll have to move to another planet," Stacie said.

Janet shivered. "That's so awful! Moda-5 is our home!"

The girls hurried up a cement walk. It led to an apartment building called Morning Star Habitat. Inside, they climbed the stairs to the second floor. Their astroboots made a loud thumping noise. A door at the top of the stairs swung open.

"Hi!" Barbie called out. "You sound like a marching army."

Stacie laughed. "A hungry army."

"Well, I have exciting news," Barbie told the girls. "So exciting that when you hear it you won't even *think* about food."

Janet shook her head. "Nothing could be *that* exciting."

Barbie led the girls into the dining room. A large star map lay open on the table. She pointed to a small planet near the middle of the map.

"This is Moda-5, in the middle of our galaxy," Barbie explained. Then she pointed to a much smaller planet at the top of the map. "And do you know what this is?"

"Nope," Stacie replied. "And I'm still starving."

Barbie smiled. "This is the planet **Rados.** It's never been explored. We know a little about it but not much. Guess who will be traveling to Rados just three days from today?"

Janet gasped. "Us?"

"Wow!" Stacie exclaimed. "My stomach just stopped grumbling!"

Barbie continued. "I got the big news today. The Junior Star Catchers Club approved our field trip."

The Junior Star Catchers Club paid for galaxy field trips. Passenger lists had to include both Modan and Human children. The trips were **educational** but were always lots of fun, too. Their purpose was to build friendships between Modans and Humans. Barbie had volunteered to help with the club.

Janet and Stacie danced around the room. "Three cheers for the Star Catchers! Rados, here we come!"

Suddenly Janet stopped dancing. She plopped down on a chair. "I just remembered something," she said. "We have to go on this trip with Modans. Yuck!"

"Double yuck!" Stacie cried, taking a seat next to Janet. "And the Modans will feel the same way about us."

Barbie listened sadly to the girls' conversation. She looked at the star map and sighed. "This galaxy is so huge," she thought. "How much of it will we need to explore before Modans and Humans learn to be friends?"

Chapter Two

Three days later, Barbie stood next to a small starship. She read the name painted on its side: *Junior Star Catchers*. "Just one hour to liftoff," she thought. "Then, at time-warp speed, we'll reach Rados in just two days. What an adventure this is going to be!"

Barbie studied the passenger and crew list. "Oh, look. A Data-Tork robot. He should come in handy," she said.

The rest of the list looked fine, too. Steve, the pilot, was a friend of Barbie's. He was in charge of the entire trip to Rados. Thorba was the

Modan copilot and astronomer. He would gather new information about the galaxy and also help Steve. Barbie would lead the exploration of Rados's rocky surface.

Trip Date: 5 / 10 / 2190
Crew:
Steve	Human/man	Starship pilot
Thorba	Modan/man	Copilot; Astronomer
Barbie	Human/woman	Geologist
Stacie	Human/girl	Student
Janet	Human/girl	Student
Franka	Modan/girl	Student
Suto	Modan/boy	Student
Data-Tork	Robot	General helpmate

CLUB JUNIOR STARCATCHERS

Barbie tucked the list into her pocket. She entered the starship to check on final preparations.

Meanwhile, Stacie and Janet were dragging a heavy supply box up the loading ramp. The girls were laughing hard and making slow progress.

The Modan children, Franka and Suto, stood quietly behind a much larger box. They focused their eyes on it and touched shoulders. The large box rose and floated up the ramp. Franka and Suto glided behind the box. They steered it into the starship's cargo bay using their minds.

"Show-offs," Stacie muttered.

Janet wiped her damp forehead with her

sleeve. "I'm thirsty. Let's get some water."

The girls found a water bottle and cups by the launchpad. They each drank a small amount of water. They noticed Suto staring at them. He looked angry.

"I know what he's thinking," declared Janet. "Modans don't get hot and thirsty when they work, like Humans. We use too much water."

"Well, it's *our* water, too," Stacie replied.

"I'm not sure Modans think so," Janet said.

An hour later, all of the crew members and passengers were aboard the starship. They strapped themselves into their seats for liftoff. Steve and Thorba sat in front of the control panel in the cockpit. Everyone else sat in the cabin area.

Barbie glanced around. Janet and Stacie were talking. Barbie could feel their excitement. Thorba was studying a star map. Franka and Suto seemed to be sitting silently. Then they both burst out laughing. They were "talking" with telepathy.

Barbie leaned back and closed her eyes. She had a strong feeling that something was missing. Did she have all her tools? Had she packed an extra pair of astroboots?

Suddenly a voice said, "I think I'm late. Please hold the gate. You've got to wait. You can't debate."

Every head turned toward the sound of the singsong voice. It came from the sleep bay. The door slid open. A short, silvery robot rolled into the cabin. It was shaped like a wide tube with a round top. And it never stopped talking.

Barbie gasped. "That's what was missing! The Data-Tork!"

The robot spun around and faced Barbie. "I'm first-rate. It's my fate. Great helpmate. I'll demonstrate. Fill my plate. Let's roller-skate."

Thorba groaned out loud. He covered his ears. "It's Dork, the Tork," he said. The man, too, spoke in a childlike Modan voice. "I've been on missions with him before. He has a loose language chip. Rap him on the back. Otherwise he'll go on **rhyming** forever!"

Dork spun around again. "Heavy weight. I tell it straight. Silver plate. Don't operate."

Steve jumped up. He crossed the cabin and gave the robot a sharp tap on the back. Finally Dork was silent.

Everyone stared at the robot and laughed.

"Attention! Attention!" said a voice over the speaker system. "This is mission control. Pilots, passengers, and ground crew, prepare for countdown in three minutes."

Steve hurried back to the cockpit. Dork clamped himself to the wall for liftoff. Everyone checked his or her seat belt and took a deep breath. The countdown began.

Ten . . . nine . . . eight . . . seven . . . six . . . five . . . four . . . three . . . two . . . one . . .
BLASTOFF!

Chapter Three

"There!" Stacie snapped a puzzle piece into position. "Another jigsaw puzzle down!"

The puzzle lay on a table in the starship cabin. All the Humans admired it. It showed a planet covered mostly with blue oceans. Odd shapes of land were scattered across the water. Above the planet were five letters: E A R T H.

"Our great-great-grandparents came from Earth," Barbie told the girls. "You finished the puzzle just in time. We land on Rados in about an hour."

Barbie walked over to where Franka and

Suto were sitting next
to a chessboard.
They were
playing chess,
but the pieces

seemed to be moving on their own. Modans played
the game using their minds to move the pieces.

Barbie sighed. Two days had gone by. She
had hoped the Modans and Humans would do
things together during the trip. Yesterday she had
suggested a hologram movie and e-darts. But the
two groups had stayed separate.

Barbie straightened her shoulders. "We'll do
better once we're on Rados," she thought. "We'll
all explore the planet together."

"Time to get ready for touchdown," Steve
called out.

Forty-five minutes later, everyone was in
position. Seat belts were fastened. All eyes were on
the cabin's video screen. The passengers watched

the starship's landing pads move toward the rocky ground. As far as they knew, no living creature had ever visited the planet Rados . . . until now!

Dork rolled across the cabin. "We're here! Give a cheer! Get the gear! All is clear!" As the robot passed Janet, she tapped him on the back.

A minute later, the cabin was hopping with activity. The Humans pulled on thick space suits and heavy boots. They strapped oxygen packs onto their backs and put on large helmets. Each helmet had a viewing window.

Before leaving Moda-5, scientists had explained to the crew what they knew about Rados. Nothing lived on the planet. Its ground temperature was 200 degrees below zero. Its atmosphere was filled with poisonous gases.

Yet the Modans needed only oxygen packs and face masks. They surrounded their bodies with energy fields. These protected them from the cold just like a space suit would.

Soon everyone was ready. They entered the airlock area. Then Steve flipped a switch. The starship door, called a hatch, opened. A ramp slid forward and touched the ground.

"Wow!" Barbie breathed. "Look at that!"

Purple mountains rose in the distance. Some were volcanoes. Orange, purple, and green gases billowed out of them. The area around the starship was flat. Black rocks of every size covered the ground. Not too far away was a large, pinkish lake.

Barbie and Thorba led the way down the ramp. Barbie suggested they head toward the lake. They would examine rocks along the way. She carried her rock kit, which contained a set of small, atomic-powered tools.

At first the Humans had trouble walking on Rados. Gravity was stronger than on Moda-5. But the Modans still glided around easily.

Barbie pointed out interesting features. They found patches of purple sand and pools of liquid

metal. The Humans used Barbie's drills and hammers. The Modans sorted rock samples. Dork saved the data. The group worked well together.

Near the lake, Barbie found a giant crack in the planet's surface. She sat down at the edge to study it. Inside, there was hard, gray rock. The rock was rough but shiny.

"I've never seen anything like this," Barbie told the others.

She used a chisel to break off a chip of rock. She put it on a slide. Then she placed it under the microscope in her kit.

"I see some tiny, strange crystals," said Barbie. "Take a look, Thorba."

Thorba bent over the microscope. "These *are* strange!" he agreed.

Barbie put another piece of rock into Dork's

study tray. She pressed the start button. Dork's system studied the rock to try and find out what was in it. Everyone crowded around. Barbie stared at Dork's computer screen. The results appeared.

"Yes! Yes! *Yes!*" Barbie shouted.

"What is it?" Steve and Janet asked together.

Barbie was breathless with excitement. She could barely speak. "Crystals! That could mean super-compressed ice."

Thorba's eyes opened wide. "Suppose the crystals *are* ice—"

"We could melt it and have water!" Steve cried.

"Then we could save Moda-5!" Suto squealed in his high voice.

Everyone began talking at once. The children jumped up and down. Dork spun around in a circle. "Moda-5 is saved! The road is paved! The flag is waved! The beard is shaved!"

Chapter Four

Barbie knocked Dork on the back. "We all have to calm down. I'm not *sure* the crystals are ice. I have to do many more tests. Let's move a supply of rocks to the starship. I'll need a core sample, too. That's a sample from deep inside the planet," she explained to the children.

"What should we do first?" Steve asked.

"Let's send Dork to the starship," Barbie suggested. "He can bring back my big tools. We'll need the atomic-powered dolly to carry the heavy rocks."

Thorba spoke up. "You don't need a machine

to move the rocks. We Modans can do it easily. We can combine our telekinetic energy. This will create a strong force."

Barbie shook her head. "I'm afraid a strong force might damage the crystals."

Thorba looked angry. "We will *not* damage anything."

Barbie thought for a moment. She didn't want to upset the Modans. Yet she had to protect the crystals. "Let's use your energy for the next batch of rocks. By then, we'll know more about them."

Thorba agreed.

Two hours later, the testing began. Barbie set up her equipment in the starship's cabin. Everyone had tasks to do. Some rocks were ground up and heated. Others were melted or frozen. Chemicals were added. Barbie looked at everything under microscopes. Thorba and Steve entered data into computers, including Dork's.

Hours slipped by. No one thought about food or rest. They couldn't wait to find out if they would be able to save Moda-5. Barbie showed **diagrams** to Thorba and Steve. They talked and talked until Barbie was ready.

"Well," said Barbie. Her eyes twinkled.

"Tell us!" Stacie begged.

"The crystals are definitely ice," Barbie stated. "But there's even more exciting news."

All the children shouted at once, "Tell us!"

"It appears that the entire core of Rados contains ice crystals," Barbie explained. "Moda-5 can ask the galaxy government for permission to set up a rock mine. We've learned to use resources more wisely on Moda-5. A small amount of these ice crystals could provide water for hundreds of years!"

The cabin shook with cheering. "Hip-hip, hooray!" they all shouted.

Dork zigzagged around the room. He was

rhyming at top speed. No one rapped him on the back. No one even noticed.

By then, everyone was tired. After a quick dinner, the children and adults climbed into their bunks in the sleep bay. Dork switched his power source to *rest and recharge*.

"What a great day," Barbie thought. Then she closed her eyes and drifted off to sleep.

*****

Ba-BEEP! Ba-BEEP! Ba-BEEP! WA-EH! WA-EH! WA-EH! BEEP-BEEP-BEEP!

Barbie sat up. She leapt out of her bunk. All the red alarm lights were flashing. She raced into the main cabin. Her mind was racing, too: "A fire? An explosion? Should we **evacuate** the starship?"

Steve, Thorba, and the children were right behind Barbie. Dork rolled toward them. All his lights were flashing, too.

"Attention! Suspension! Prevention! Detention!" Dork exclaimed.

Steve rapped Dork on the back and entered the cockpit. He worked at the control panel for several minutes. The alarm system shut off.

"The starship is okay," Steve told them. "But something else is going on. An invisible force seems to be pulling on the planet. As the astronomer, Thorba should look at the data."

Thorba sat down at the control panel. He studied the computer and radar screens. He pressed buttons. He flipped switches. Everyone else stood behind him and waited.

Finally Thorba turned around. His purple face had turned pale. "The planet Rados has been pulled out of its normal orbit," he stated. "That's what set off our alarms."

"What could possibly pull a planet?" Barbie wondered.

Thorba took a deep breath. "Rados is being sucked into a black hole!"

Chapter Five

"Sucked into a black hole!" Stacie repeated.

"Are we getting sucked in, too?" Suto cried.

"Nothing escapes a black hole," Franka declared, "not even light!"

"Maybe we should go home," suggested Janet. "Now!"

"Please don't worry," Thorba pleaded. "Our starship isn't in danger." The Modan man's childlike voice sounded soft and calm. It made all of the children feel better.

"Our starship can blast away from the black hole," the Modan girl said. "We can use our rockets."

"But Rados is a planet," Suto pointed out. "It doesn't have rockets. How can we stop it from getting sucked in?"

Thorba shook his head. "A black hole is a force of nature. We can't stop such a huge force."

"But what about the ice crystals?" Steve reminded him. "Moda-5 needs the water."

"Can't we mine some of the rocks *before* Rados disappears?" Barbie asked. "How much time is left? We only need a few weeks."

"It depends on the strength of the black hole," Thorba explained. "A stronger force pulls faster. And the closer you get to a black hole, the faster it pulls things in. It's like water going down the bathtub drain. When the water gets closer to the drain, *whoosh!* It gets sucked in faster."

Steve spoke up. "Why don't we measure the force of the black hole?" he suggested. "Then we'll know when Rados will disappear."

Thorba thought for a moment. "There's

only one way to do that. We must move closer and closer to the black hole. As we move, we can measure the growing force."

"Would we do this in the starship?" Barbie asked Steve, the ship's pilot.

"No, it's too big and hard to handle," he answered. "We'll need to use the space pod." The space pod was a tiny spaceship used for short trips. It was stored inside the starship.

Stacie looked worried. "Won't the space pod get sucked into the black hole, too?"

"No," Thorba replied. "Imagine this: Tie a ball to one end of a string. Then hold the other end. Whirl the ball around in a circle over your head. If you keep up the speed of the whirling, the ball won't fall. Now imagine the ball is our space pod. We'll fly to the black hole and then circle it over and over again, very fast. That way, we won't get sucked in."

Barbie looked out the cockpit window. It was

nighttime on Rados. Far across the galaxy, it was also nighttime on Moda-5. The two planets were so different. There was no life on Rados. Yet Rados could help save life on Moda-5.

Barbie turned to the others. "Let's do it! Let's head for the black hole!"

"Yes!" agreed Steve, Stacie, and Janet.

The Modans stared at one another. Using telepathy, they discussed the idea. When they finished, they all nodded "yes" as well.

Then Thorba spoke out loud. "We think the Modans should pilot the space pod. We know how to work with energy forces. The Humans could take charge of the starship."

"That's not fair," Stacie protested. "We want to be in the space pod, too. The Humans can handle the controls better."

Dork spun around. "What's fair? Should we care? Split the hair. Do you dare?"

"Wait a minute," Barbie broke in. She gave

Dork a tap. "We need Modan talents *and* Human talents. A mixed crew is our best bet. Okay?"

Everyone looked at one another and nodded. Barbie breathed a sigh of relief.

Soon the mission began. The starship left Rados and headed toward the black hole. At a safe distance, Steve put the starship into orbit around the black hole. The space pod crew went over their plans. Thorba would pilot the space pod. Barbie would copilot. Stacie and Franka would collect the data. Steve would direct the mission from the starship. Janet, Suto, and Dork would stay with Steve to help.

The space pod crew was ready. Each person lined up in front of a narrow hatch. It led right into the space pod. They looked a little nervous. New space missions could be dangerous.

The hatch slid open. One by one, the crew stepped into the space pod. Dork's voice sounded very low. "Worry. Hurry. Scurry. Flurry."

Chapter Six

"Ready for rockets," Barbie said. "Now!"

Inside the space pod, Thorba fired a set of rockets. The force of the rockets pushed the space pod away from the starship. Thorba steered closer to the black hole. He kept his eyes on the control panel. Barbie sat next to him, watching the radar screen.

"Ready for rockets," Barbie repeated. "Now!"

Thorba fired a second set of rockets. The space pod lurched forward. Thorba moved it into a new orbit that was closer to the black hole. They were moving faster now. The speed of the new orbit would keep the capsule from getting sucked into the black hole. They were closer to the hole, but still safe.

Stacie and Franka sat behind Thorba and Barbie. Stacie held a small remote-control unit. She waited for Franka's signal.

"Ready to release probe," Franka said. "Now!"

Stacie pressed a button. A tube-shaped probe dropped from the space pod. The probe helped measure the pulling force of the black hole. As it fell, it sent data back to the space pod's computer. Then the probe was sucked into the black hole.

Thorba and Barbie looked at the data on the computer.

"Ready to drop to the next level of orbit," Barbie said. "Now!"

Once again, Thorba let the space pod drop closer to the black hole. Barbie gave him the signal to fire the rockets. Thorba shifted the space pod into a new orbit. Franka gave the signal to

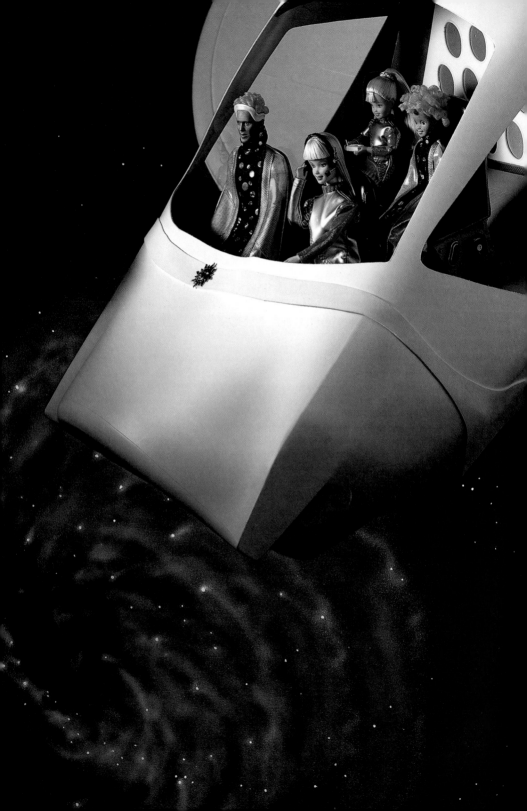

release another probe.

The space pod dropped one, two, three, four levels. On each level, Thorba and Barbie looked at the data. They began to worry.

"Okay, once more," Thorba instructed.

The space pod dropped a fifth time. Through the window, everyone saw the black hole. It was below them. A cloud of gases and dust swirled around and around. At its center was the pitch-black hole.

Thorba stopped the capsule from moving farther down. Then he put the capsule into orbit. Another probe dropped down. Barbie and Thorba stared at the computer.

"Uh-oh," Barbie murmured. "This doesn't look good."

Thorba shook his head. "It's really *bad*," he agreed. "Rados will be sucked into the black hole in just twenty hours!"

"Good-bye, water," Barbie said with a sigh.

"There's nothing we can do to save Rados. We'd better get back to the starship. Ready, Thorba?"

But Thorba didn't answer. Barbie looked at him. The Modan man sat as still as a statue.

"Thorba!" Barbie shouted. She touched Thorba's shoulder. She pressed her fingers against his wrist. Thorba didn't move. His pulse was steady but slow. Just as Barbie turned around, Stacie gasped.

"Barbie!" Stacie cried. "Franka's frozen! She's not even blinking!"

The Modan girl sat as still as Thorba. Barbie felt her pulse. It was the same as Thorba's. Then Barbie checked the control panel. The pod was in a safe orbit. Something was affecting the Modans, but not the Humans.

Barbie squeezed her sister's hand. "Don't worry. Everything will be okay. The black hole's energy is doing something to Franka and Thorba. We'll move away from it. We just need to return to the starship."

Barbie and Steve spoke by radio. Then Barbie showed Stacie how to help her navigate.

"Ready? Here we go," Barbie told her sister.

Barbie fired the rockets. The pod rose into the vast space above the black hole. Slowly and carefully, Barbie moved up from one level to the next.

Steve's voice came over the radio. "You're doing a great job, Barbie and Stacie!"

Barbie fired the rockets one more time. The space pod rose higher and higher. Finally it reached the level of the starship.

"Docking now," Barbie said into her headset.

With a loud click, the two ships locked together. Barbie shut down the controls. A moment later, the hatch slid open. Steve, Suto, and Janet rushed in. They gently carried Thorba and Franka to the starship's sick bay, which was like a one-room hospital.

Thorba and Franka lay on examining tables. Though their eyes were open, they seemed to be in a deep sleep.

Dork checked for changes in their breathing. "Deep sleep. Not a peep. Counting sheep," he whispered.

"They seem to be in some kind of energy shock," Barbie guessed.

Suto nodded. "I'm going to wrap them in a force field. It will be like a healing blanket." He stood nearby and stared at his fellow Modans.

The Humans couldn't see the force field, but they noticed Franka's shoulders move. Then Thorba's lips twitched.

"Can you hear me?" Barbie asked softly.

The two Modans nodded. Thorba smiled a little. "Good job getting us back, Barbie," he said.

Bit by bit, Thorba and Franka returned to normal. They moved their heads. They sat up. Suto removed the force field and gave them some

vita juice. Thorba wanted to move to the main cabin. The others insisted on carrying them there. Everyone settled into soft chairs. Franka and Thorba said they felt fine. According to Dork's data, they *were* fine.

It was time to decide what to do next. No one knew how to save Rados.

"We'd better head home to Moda-5," Steve finally said.

"Without the crystals," Stacie added.

"At least we tried," Franka pointed out.

WHOOSH! A can of vita juice shot across the cabin.

Janet ducked just in time. "What in the cosmos was *that?*" she exclaimed.

"I was just getting myself some juice," Franka

answered. "I used telekinesis the way I always do. But the can moved really fast."

Everyone was puzzled.

"I'd better go enter this into my data book," Thorba said.

WHOOSH! Thorba flew across the cabin. He landed in the desk chair. *WHOOSH!* The data book came flying toward him. It landed in his lap.

Dork spun around. "Oh, my. Books fly. Don't cry. Find out why."

Barbie rapped Dork on the back. "What's going on?"

Thorba looked stunned. "I meant to float myself slowly to this chair. I wanted to sit at the desk and work on the data book."

The cabin grew quiet. Everyone was thinking.

Finally Stacie spoke up. "When Franka and Thorba try to do something small, it turns into something big," she commented.

"Yeah," Janet agreed. "It's as if they have

too much energy. They seem supercharged or something."

"You're right!" Thorba stated. "Modans are like batteries. We store up energy. I wonder if the black hole supercharged us. Maybe I can measure this energy with Dork's help."

Dork rolled toward Thorba. "Here I come. I'll find the sum. I'm not dumb. I'm your chum."

Thorba stared at Dork's power meter. He sent the tiniest energy beam toward it. Dork's body shook. Hundreds of numbers flew across his computer screen.

"Wow!" Thorba exclaimed. "I've stored up three thousand times my normal energy! The same must be true for Franka."

Everyone thought about this amazing news. Then two voices broke the silence. One voice was Human. The other was Modan. They spoke the same words: "We can save Rados!"

Chapter Seven

Barbie and Thorba had come up with the same idea. Barbie explained the plan to the others.

Stacie, Barbie, and Suto would take the space pod down toward the black hole. They would stop at the point where Thorba and Franka had "frozen." Suto would become supercharged there. Then they would return to the ship. The three Modans would combine their supercharged forces. They would aim this giant force at the planet Rados. Together, their huge force would push the planet back into a safe orbit.

"It's worth a try," Thorba said.

Everyone agreed. No one argued about what Humans or Modans should do. Each group had its own necessary job.

An hour later, the space pod was once again dropping toward the black hole. Barbie and Stacie sat at the control panel. Suto sat behind them. At the fifth level, Suto became as still as a statue. Barbie piloted the pod back to the orbiting starship. When Suto awakened, he felt fine.

"So far, so good," Barbie said.

Then Steve piloted the starship toward Rados. He stopped close to the planet. The black hole, the starship, and the planet were in a straight line.

"Everything's set," Steve said. "The Humans should carry the Modans into the cockpit. That way, they won't go flying around the cabin."

In the cockpit, Steve watched the radar screen. The Modans stood side by side. They faced the large window over the control panel. They stared at Rados, waiting for Steve's signal.

"Now!" he called.

The Modans touched shoulders. Without a word, they combined their energy forces into one beam. They hurled it at Rados.

Barbie peeked over Steve's shoulder at the radar screen. "Rados is moving!" she cried. She watched the planet move slowly. It moved away from the starship and the black hole. The minutes passed. Everyone was silent.

"Stop!" Steve called out suddenly.

The three Modans moved apart and sank into chairs. Their extra energy was drained. Janet and Stacie brought them cans of vita juice.

After a few sips, Thorba rose. He floated calmly to the radar screen. He studied it for several minutes and smiled. "Perfect! Rados has a new and safe orbit!"

Once again, the starship rang with the sound of cheering. Dork's lights began flashing. "Just dandy! Really handy! Sugar candy!"

The starship took off through the galaxy at time-warp speed. Everyone was tired but happy.

"Wait until the Junior Star Catchers Club hears about us!" Stacie exclaimed. "We started out on a field trip to explore Rados—"

"And we ended up saving life on Moda-5!" Franka finished. "Won't it be great when everyone in the galaxy neighborhood knows?"

Barbie told them, "I just gave a full report to mission control on Moda-5. Tomorrow morning we'll be front-page news in *The Moda Times* and *The Planetary Post!*"

Barbie sat down. She closed her eyes and listened to everyone talk. The Modans were chatting out loud with the Humans. No one seemed to notice anyone's accent. "They sound just like old friends," Barbie thought. "Mission accomplished."

"Barbie," Suto called, "are you falling asleep?"

"Not yet," Barbie replied. "I'm too excited."

"We are, too," the Modan boy said. "Let's all watch a hologram movie together."

Barbie opened her eyes. "Sounds super to me."

*****

Stacie looked up at the sun-star in the sky. She was standing on a platform in Cosmos Plaza. The platform was next to the dry fountain. All her friends from the starship were there, too. So was the council leader of Moda-5. Ten thousand Modans and Humans crowded into the plaza.

One month had passed since the starship had returned home. A new water plant had been built. Many tons of rock had already arrived from Rados to be processed into life-giving water. Another important change had taken place. Stacie, Janet, Suto, and Franka had become good friends at school. They were even doing a project together on black holes.

The council leader of Moda-5 stepped forward. "Welcome, everyone," she began. "I just want to thank these brave citizens from the Junior Star Catchers Club for making this day possible. I also want to thank the Club itself for its great work. Lastly, I want to thank you, the people of Moda-5. I believe we have learned how precious our resources are and how to protect them. Even this fountain has been redesigned to do that. I am proud of all of us."

The council leader nodded at Barbie and Thorba. They were standing next to a large switch. Barbie placed her hand on it. Thorba stared at it. Together they flipped the switch.

There was a deep rumbling sound beneath the ground. *Gurgle! Gurgle! SPLASH!* Water gushed into the fountain. Ten thousand people cheered.

Barbie smiled when she heard a familiar sound. It was Dork spinning around.

"Hole was black. What a knack. Ticky-tack. Lost the track. Tap my back. *Please!*"